Life Cycles

Butterflies

Maria Koran

EYEDISCOVER

EYEDISCOVER

Go to **www.eyediscover.com** and enter this book's unique code.

BOOK CODE

U587868

EYEDISCOVER brings you optic readalongs that support active learning.

Published by AV² by Weigl
350 5th Avenue, 59th Floor   New York, NY   10118
Website: www.eyediscover.com

Library of Congress Control Number: 2016946717

ISBN 978-1-4896-5335-2 (hardcover)

Printed in the United States of America
in Brainerd, Minnesota
1 2 3 4 5 6 7 8 9 0   20 19 18 17 16

072016
040716

Project Coordinator: Warren Rylands
Designer: Mandy Christiansen

Weigl acknowledges Getty Images, Corbis, and iStock as the primary image suppliers for this title.

EYEDISCOVER provides enriched content, optimized for tablet use, that supplements and complements this book. EYEDISCOVER books strive to create inspired learning and engage young minds in a total learning experience.

I am a lion.

Watch
Video content brings each page to life.

Browse
Thumbnails make navigation simple.

Read
Follow along with text on the screen.

Listen
Hear each page read aloud.

Your EYEDISCOVER Optic Readalongs come alive with...

Audio
Listen to the entire book read aloud.

Video
High resolution videos turn each spread into an optic readalong.

OPTIMIZED FOR

✔ **TABLETS**

✔ **WHITEBOARDS**

✔ **COMPUTERS**

✔ **AND MUCH MORE!**

Life Cycles
Butterflies

In this book, you will learn about

- how I look

- where I live

- what I do

and much more!

The stages a living thing goes through during its life are called its life cycle. Let's explore a butterfly's life cycle.

5

6

Butterflies hatch from eggs when they are born. They eat a hole in the egg to get out.

Baby butterflies look like worms with legs. They are called caterpillars.

10

Caterpillars eat a lot and grow fast. They turn into larvae when they grow too big for their skin.

Caterpillars attach themselves to a branch when they are fully grown. This is the pupa stage of the life cycle.

13

14

The butterfly forms inside a shell. When it comes out of this shell, the butterfly is fully grown.

Butterflies can fly only a few hours after leaving their shells. Their soft wings become hard.

17

18

Butterflies can lay eggs soon after they start to fly. Their eggs are often placed on leaves with special glue to keep them safe.

Butterflies are insects. Like all insects, they have three body parts.

21

BUTTERFLIES BY THE NUMBERS

Butterflies **taste with their feet.**

A butterfly's eggs may be **round, oval,** or **tube-shaped.**

There are **24,000** different kinds of **butterflies** on Earth.

Most butterflies fly at speeds of 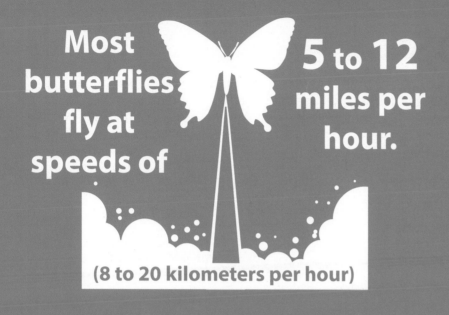 **5 to 12** miles per hour.

(8 to 20 kilometers per hour)

A caterpillar can eat an entire leaf in **one hour**.

Butterflies **can not fly** if they are cold.

Butterflies live on an **all-liquid** diet.

KEY WORDS

Research has shown that as much as 65 percent of all written material published in English is made up of 300 words. These 300 words cannot be taught using pictures or learned by sounding them out. They must be recognized by sight. This book contains 49 common sight words to help young readers improve their reading fluency and comprehension. This book also teaches young readers several important content words, such as proper nouns. These words are paired with pictures to aid in learning and improve understanding.

Page	Sight Words First Appearance
4	a, are, its, let, life, the, thing, through
7	eat, from, get, in, out, they, to, when
8	like, look, with
11	and, big, for, grow, into, their, too, turn
12	is, of, this
15	comes, it
16	after, can, few, hard, only
19	keep, leaves, often, on, placed, soon, start, them
20	all, have, parts, three

Page	Content Words First Appearance
4	butterfly, life cycle, stages
7	eggs, hole
8	caterpillars, legs, worms
11	larvae, skin
12	branch, pupa stage
15	shell
16	hours, wings
19	glue
20	insects

I am a lion.

Watch
Video content brings each page to life.

Browse
Thumbnails make navigation simple.

Read
Follow along with text on the screen.

Listen
Hear each page read aloud.

EYEDISCOVER

Go to www.eyediscover.com and enter this book's unique code.

BOOK CODE

U587868